Murder by the Scoopful

An Ice Cream Truck Mystery
Book 2

Virginia K. Bennett

To: Lauren & Lindsey

Virginia K. Bennett

To the members of the writing community who supported me early on, thank you!

Skye Jones
Marissa Farrar
Dawn Edwards
Kat Reads Romance
Kathryn LeBlanc
TL Swan
VR Tennent
Gina Sturino
Rachelle Kampen
...and so many more!

Table of Contents

Chapter 1

The Commute

"It was so good to meet you all," Katie said as she entered the driver's side of her pink ice cream truck. "I'd love to come back next year, if you'll have me."

"It would be our pleasure," replied the lifeguard.

Katie had been traveling around the state of Maine for the past month or so, learning the ropes of running and living in an ice cream truck that doubled as her home. Just having finished an extended-weekend gig supplying ice cream to lifeguards on a busy stretch of beach, she was getting ready to pack up and move on to her next destination.

"Pass that recommendation on to your boss, please. I so want to do this again." She closed the door and rolled down the window. "See you next year." A wave was the final goodbye as she pulled out of the parking spot adjacent to the lifeguard station. Several lifeguards waved and whistled as she drove away, Jaspurr watching out the windshield from his harnessed perch.

"Jaspurr, are you ready to head to New Hampshire? I imagine it won't be all that different from Maine, though there's a lot less coastline."

The orange cat let out a small bark—not a meow—responding in a way that neither confirmed nor denied his agreement. Jaspurr had learned to love his front-seat adventures around Maine, so Katie assumed he'd enjoy New Hampshire just as much.

The ice cream truck Katie acquired in May had become their permanent residence as of June first. It wasn't always possible to find an arrangement like the retirement home she started at, so a generator was her first major purchase after the truck itself. Once she had enough money, the second purchase was a locking rooftop cargo carrier. While it was possible to store all of her warm-weather gear in the bed area, everything took up more space as the temperature got cooler, and there was no doubt it would get cooler come fall.

Katie stopped first at a campground where she would be able to plug in her truck and take a real shower. The visit was only from Tuesday afternoon to Wednesday afternoon, because she was due to be parked in her new location before bedtime Wednesday night. When she got settled, she found where to do all of her laundry, taking Jaspurr out for a walk as soon as both loads were running. The outfit she had remaining was actually a pajama set, but she was confident no one would notice.

Her truck was parked one spot away from a secluded beach and pavilion no one was using, presumably because it was the middle of the week. She had a bath-room, with toilets and sinks only, close by, but she wasn't complaining about that. Jaspurr happily took the tour of the campground on his harness and leash, strutting with his head up and chest puffed out for all to see.

"Sweetie, I think I'll take a dip in the pond later. Guessing you won't want to join me for that."

Jaspurr sneezed and shook his head.

"I'll take that as a no, but if I'm wrong, just let me know."

Katie and Jaspurr continued to walk around the campground, making a complete trip around the pond. When they returned to the truck, ready for a good night of sleep away from traffic noise, she found the director of the campground waiting for her.

"Good evening, Katie. I'm Director Evie, and I was wondering if I might bend your ear for a minute or two."

Always one for a chat, she nodded. "Let me grab my camp chairs."

"Oh, I don't need a chair. This will be quick. I noticed when you drove in that this was an ice cream truck."

Katie picked up Jaspurr, still wearing his harness and leash. "That it is." She gestured to the signage painted on the truck.

"Well, I was wondering if you might want to set up tomorrow in the campground to sell ice cream. We're hoping to not have any kind of fee to set up, and we'll waive tonight's overnight charge in exchange." She held

3

up crossed fingers. "We have a summer camp, and it would be a great surprise to have you here after lunch."

She thought for a moment. "Do you know how much longer of a drive I have until I reach Lebanon? I'm due to be there tomorrow before five to get my permits with the city settled."

"Well, if we can have you finished by half past two, that would give you plenty of time to get to Lebanon before five. Do we have a deal?" Even though Katie hadn't answered, Evie was nodding furiously, trying to sway Katie's decision in her direction.

"I left my last gig with plenty of supplies, so I don't see why not." She knew of a place where she could restock near Lebanon, so she'd be all set for a Thursday start should the campers wipe her out.

"That's settled. Can you be set up and ready to serve by noon? Some campers eat as early as eleven, and we'll want to stagger them."

"I can, just tell me where."

The two women discussed the parameters for how much each camper could have as the camp would be paying for the product. The campground preferred to have people follow a carry-in/carry-out procedure but understood that taking care of the waste from the event would be their responsibility.

"And what about the camp counselors? They'll get ice cream too, right?"

"Of course. They can get the size up, and we'll cover that too."

"I'll only charge you for the small for everyone, but

4

I'll give them more. Camp counselor is kinda like being a teacher. Everyone needs you, but no one remembers just how hard you work."

Evie concurred by exhaling a large sigh. "You can say that again." Katie almost started to say it again when Evie blurted, "Well, good night." She quickly did an about face and took off in the direction of the entrance to the camp.

"Well, Jaspurr, that worked out nicely. Always happy to land a job just because the truck does the work for me. We'll be on their dime, make some money, save some money and still get to the next location on time. What could be better?" She nuzzled noses with Jaspurr before removing the harness and placing him in the passenger seat of the truck. "I'll be back soon." She grabbed the toiletry bag, including the reserved change of clothes and her remaining clean towel, and headed to the bath house.

The shower was warm, and the floor was clean, though she kept her plastic flip flops on just in case. According to the time, her clothes were ready to go in the dryer, so she made that detour on the way back to snuggle Jaspurr. She figured since they locked the laundry room in fifteen minutes, she'd just get there when it opened to pick up the dry clothes tomorrow morning.

When she snuggled Jaspurr in the loft bed of her ice cream truck that summer Tuesday night, even if she was warm and wishing for air conditioning instead of a fan and skylight, she knew that Katie Thorne was living exactly the life she wanted.

Morning came quickly, and her phone alarm let her

know she needed to go collect her clothes in the next ten minutes.

"Jaspurr, let's get you outside for a walk so we can pick up clean clothes, sheets and towels. You with me?" An affectionate head bump to the shoulder let her know he was ready. He jumped down from the loft bed before she could descend the retractable stairs and slipped on his harness that Katie left for him on the passenger-side freezer last night. She reached the floor of the truck, attached the buckles on the harness and stepped out the back door.

Still in the same pajama set as last night, she crossed the campground, the pebbles under her flip flops and birds the only sounds. She had thrown a Red Sox cap on to cover her messy bedhead until she could wash her hair again, not willing to let a good shower go to waste — depending on time, she might even shower once more before leaving.

She set down her collapsable basket when she entered the laundry room, Jaspurr inside. She wasn't about to get in trouble for allowing him on the folding table. She folded the laundry mid-air, placing items next to Jaspurr in the basket. When it was half full of folded sheets and towels, Jaspurr transferred to the top of the pile, leaving room in the other half for the remaining load of clothes.

"Thank you, little man. You're so considerate." She finished the folding and carried the basket back outside, allowing Jaspurr to jump down once the door had closed behind her.

The morning was full of chores that made the truck livable. For about a week, she could just wing it, but soon after, she needed an extended deep dive in cleaning and tidying. The freezers were organized and signage updated. Katie mopped the floor in the back and used a hand-held vacuum to clean the front seats and floor. She had a hard time believing this small space could take so long to clean with just one human and one cat.

"Jaspurr, need another walk before work?" He jumped down from the front seat where he had been curled up, leapt to the freezer then the loft bed where he curled up in the opposite direction. "Guess not." She put up the mesh barrier, restricting Jaspurr to this area of the truck while she worked.

Katie unplugged the truck and packed everything in its assigned location before backing out and relocating to the serving area. At five minutes to noon, she was in place with the window open, awning up and flavor board in place. Director Evie came running up in a panic.

"Are you all set? Do you need anything? The first fifty campers will be here any moment."

"Evie, I'm ready for them. Don't you worry."

She put her hands on the serving counter and dropped her head between her arms. "Sorry, but I don't often find people to be that reliable."

"I'm here as your trusty ice cream scooper to restore your faith in humanity." Katie assumed a superhero pose as if her red cape was blowing in the wind behind her. Evie laughed. "Bring it on."

"Will do."

With a menu of only six flavors available to stream-line the process, Katie was a super scooper, handing out Cookies & Cream of the Crop, Chocolate Mudslide, Granite Toffee Crunch, Mint Chocolate Chip off the Old Block, Strawberry Fields Forever and Very Vanilla — Vivid Vanilla seemed a bit extra for a summer camp of kids. Some wanted bowls while most wanted sugar cones. The plain cone was practically neglected, like she expected. Between groups, Katie checked on Jaspurr, living up to the cat average of thirteen to sixteen hours of sleep per day.

When she looked at the clock and realized it was after two and there was still a line of kids in front of her, she sent for a counselor to find Evie.

"Hey, Evie, I thought you said I'd be done in time to get to Lebanon before five. How close am I cutting it?"

"As long as you're out of here in the next thirty minutes, you'll be good to go."

Katie kept scooping as kids asked for their desired flavor. "Can you figure out the payment based on the number I've already served and what's left in this line so I can go as soon as possible?"

Evie counted heads and returned to the window. "What's the already-served count?"

Katie checked her sheet of tally marks. "Three hundred twenty-two." Her arm and wrist felt like it was even more.

"I've got you covered." Evie took off, returning about fifteen minutes later as the line was almost done. "I can't thank you enough. Payment is in cash. I counted it twice to make sure, but I won't be offended if you triple check. Didn't want you to have to wait to cash it if you don't have a bank around here. We really appreciate you working on an off day, don't we kids?" She shouted the last three words, raising a cheer from the last group of about seventy teenage campers. Since it was over eighty degrees, Katie guessed most of their enthusiasm was authentic.

"Keep me in mind if you want to book visits in the future. Mid-week is easy if I'm in the area."

"We will, and if you need a place to stop on your way through, keep us in mind."

Katie started to clean the counter and freezers immediately, knowing she needed to get on the road. "Can I leave the truck here, locked up of course, long enough to wash off the used utensils?"

"Not a problem. I'll keep a counselor here to watch the truck. I know you've got Jaspurr in there. He's safe with us."

Katie closed the window and rushed outside to take down the awning. The truck was locked up in a flash as she sped to the bath house with a wash tub and soap. Setting them on the edge of the sink counter, she jumped in a shower stall and took the fastest rinse possible, making sure to wash her hair and body with the available free soap. She put the same clothes back on, figuring she'd brush her hair back at the truck, and cleaned the utensils thoroughly before returning. The clock told her she had two minutes left to be 'on time.'

The counselors held the campers back as she turned

the truck around and pulled — slowly — out of the camp-ground bound for Lebanon.

Chapter 2

The Logistics

KATIE TRAVELED ACROSS THE REST OF NEW Hampshire on Route 4, passing through small town after small town. The lack of highways going west to east didn't bother her because she enjoyed driving at slower speeds and seeing what new areas had to offer. Jaspurr, on the other hand, slept on his side of the truck for the extended drive.

When she finally started to see signs for Lebanon, she got excited to see if the city lived up to everything she had created in her head. The woman she talked to at the town offices, Linda, told her to park behind City Hall and gave her good directions for the final few minutes of the drive. Katie had less than a half hour to make sure she got her permits in place for her four-night stay in the City of Fountains.

She parked her ice cream truck in an area that had plenty of available space, since she took up at least two spots when parking accurately — four spots on a bad day. The instructions for how to get into the building were detailed, which she appreciated. The cool air felt amazing, even after just a few hundred feet of walking. The line only had one person in front of her, so she was optimistic.

With five minutes to spare, Katie walked out of the town office with all her paperwork squared away. She returned to the trunk, Jaspurr still sleeping on the front seat with the air conditioning running, and followed the directions to get to the spot she was allowed to park until Sunday. The tricky part was getting around a road that was closed off to allow a restaurant to have outdoor seating during the summer. Crisis averted, she parked in the designated spaces for food trucks.

It was Wednesday, and her selling permit was good from Thursday through Sunday, so today she could explore what they called 'The Green' and 'The Mall' on foot. If she learned of anything else cool to check out, it would need to wait until Friday evening at the earliest. She did some research — which meant she spent some time on Google — and learned there was an ice cream shop a short walk from where she was parked, so she'd have to gauge her hours off the popularity of the other location once she got a feel for it.

Her reason for choosing Lebanon was their farmers' market on Thursdays. It seemed to Katie that there had been more and more food trucks gravitating to the area — based on "research" — and she wanted to be part of the trend. If it was worthwhile, she'd make another pass or two during the summer.

Katie rattled Jaspurr's harness and leash. He lifted his head, probably checking that she was actually holding the leash and not just shaking it on the hook behind the driver's seat. When the appropriate results had been observed, Jaspurr stretched out his front paws as far and wide as he could, subsequently sticking his rear end and tail as high as possible in the opposite direction. Once thoroughly stretched, he did a single hop into Katie's lap.

"Let's get out of this truck and put some miles on our legs." She lifted him after securing the harness and exited the truck, happy to be able to focus on their comfort and relaxation before another busy day tomorrow.

It was hard for her to believe that she'd worked a significant and unplanned shift today at the campground. The first order of business was for Jaspurr to do his business. It wasn't quite the same for a cat as it was walking a dog, but Katie came prepared with bags to clean up after him. Katie finding a bathroom, however, was usually a little more difficult. She had been smart enough to use the facilities in the town office so she wouldn't need to worry about taking Jaspurr into a business.

Once Jaspurr was all set, they made their way across the park, known to locals as The Green, where the farmers' market would turn this quiet stretch of grass into a bustling marketplace. The fountain in the center of the park was only the first of many fountains she hoped to see on her working visit to Lebanon. Katie's destination was an Italian restaurant, the one with the outdoor seating in the street. She acquired a table for two and set up a collapsable bowl of water under the table. Jaspurr was more than happy sitting under the table, watching for bugs and anything else that moved. He'd bark in the way only an orange cat could bark, but never pull on the leash to actually attack.

The waitress approached several times to hand her a menu, take her order, fill her water, deliver her order and clean up after the meal, each time with a pleasant demeanor. She was surprised to find Katie had a cat under the table and not a dog.

"That's a first," she said as she brought the bill. "I've never seen a cat at the table before."

"He travels with me in my ice cream truck, so we have to get creative when I go out to eat."

"Well, he was a perfect dinner guest." Katie already knew that but thanked her for the compliment.

They left dinner, passing by a newly renovated fountain, only to find the cookie shop she hoped to visit was already closed. Since Katie planned to get into town earlier, it shouldn't have been a problem. Prioritizing a visit would have to make her short list for tomorrow. The cookie shop was one of several businesses on 'The Mall.' There was a section of what might have once been an operational street but was now exclusively for foot traffic, though it did boast a bike shop. There were other small storefronts as well as access to different buildings with offices for all types of professionals. Katie walked Jaspurr to the end, then all around town, wherever she felt the evening took her.

At one point, Jaspurr seemed to be pulling on the leash, hesitant to walk, so she picked him up. "Did the walk get a little too long for you?" she asked, and he rubbed his face along her cheek, placing his front legs over her shoulder. "We can head back for the night."

She was glad she had picked Jaspurr up for the remaining walk back to the truck because it was uphill. She turned the truck on for a bit to get the space cooled off some. Though the generator had been running for the freezers, it didn't do anything for their sleeping space. Katie knew she wasn't technically allowed to sleep in the truck, so she made sure to put up privacy panels around the front windows.

"Tomorrow, Jaspurr, we'll get to see what the Lebanon Farmers' Market really looks like."

After a comfortable night of sleep — as comfortable as a loft bed in a hot truck could be — Katie got up and put a sign out at the front of the truck stating that their hours started at two in the afternoon. She wanted to get a day pass for the local gym and check out the cookie place. It was early in the morning, so she left the truck in it's spot, choosing to walk to the gym for a shower before, what she predicted could be, a very busy day.

Jaspurr got out for a quick walk before curling back up on the loft bed, assuming his rightful spot on Katie's pillow. Her trip to the gym was going to be brief so he wasn't alone for too long. If she was lucky, she'd be able to close up at the end of the market and still get in another shower that night on the same pass. She threw a sling bag on her back with a towel, change of clothes and her toiletries.

When she arrived, the lovely woman behind the desk greeted her. "Good morning. Checking in?"

"I'm looking for a day pass. Just in town for a brief visit, and this place was recommended online."

"Well, I'd be happy to take your picture and get things started. Name's Ingrid, and I'm new here, so give me just a second." She dug around behind the counter, her similar short haircut only different from Katie's because of her gray color. "Got it." She handed Katie a form to fill out. When it was complete, Ingrid took Katie's picture and accepted payment for the day pass. "You can use the entire facility. We have some classes and equipment that require an orientation, so just ask a fitness instructor for details. Any questions?"

"None that I can think of, Ingrid. Have a nice day."

Katie went straight for the locker room. The sandals she wore over for the walk would double as shower shoes. She wasted no time getting washed up and dressed before heading back out again with wet hair — it dried quickly being above the shoulder and fine.

"Ma'am, is there something wrong?" Ingrid asked as Katie was about to leave.

"Nothing's wrong. Why do you ask?"

Ingrid looked at her watch then checked the clock on the wall. "You only just got here less than thirty minutes ago. Did you find the facility not to your liking?"

"Everything was fine. I needed a place to shower and

get ready for the day. This fit the bill. I run an ice cream truck, and I'm stationed on The Green for the farmers' market tonight. I hope to see you there."

"Do you have any flyers? I'm sure the manager would let you leave them on the desk."

Ingrid gave off grandmotherly vibes, like someone who would do anything to help her fellow human.

"I don't, but feel free to spread the word." Katie waved as she left. She didn't want to come off as rude, but she also didn't want to leave Jaspurr in the truck too long.

When she got back to the truck, there was a police officer waiting for her. Now wishing she had taken the time to dry her hair, Katie attempted to finger comb it into something more presentable.

"Good morning, Officer..." She squinted, trying to read the name on the badge.

"Beauregard. Officer Beauregard. Ma'am, can I see your permit to park this here truck and operate your mobile business?" He pronounced mobile so that it rhymed with style instead of global, emphasizing the second syllable.

"Of course, Officer Beauregard. Have I done something wrong?" She opened the passenger door, hoping Jaspurr wasn't right there. The privacy panels were wonderful when you were inside the truck, but they made things difficult when there might be a cat waiting to leap out if you weren't quick enough.

"Depends if you have the paperwork. You are expected to display it in the windshield when parked here." Using a pen, he motioned to the side of the road posted for food trucks.

"I'm so sorry. I wasn't open, so I figured I didn't need it out yet. I'm terribly sorry." She grabbed the paperwork with no sign of Jaspurr.

He looked over the documents, apparently finding them to be in good order. "Now, this is the page we should be able to see at all times when parked here. Thank you for being so cooperative."

"Not a problem at all, Officer. Sorry I wasted your time. I'm here Thursday through Sunday, like it says on the paperwork." Katie was starting to feel heat creep up her neck and cheeks. Officer Beauregard was very handsome, but it wasn't typical for her to get affected like this.

"No time wasted. So, you'll be open for the market. I'll cross my fingers as long as you don't spill the salt."

She didn't quite know what to make of the salt comment. "Should I have a lot of competition?"

He pointed to the other side of the street. "There's a Sno-Cone trailer that pulls up there, and they've been pretty popular. Hopefully they're not too cutthroat." He laughed, as if he had made the funniest joke — it wasn't even an ice cream joke.

"Well, I hope you have a great day." She was hoping to get Jaspurr soon and make her way to Rookie's Cookies. "Maybe I'll see you later tonight." She walked around to the driver's side, hoping he would take the hint to move on.

"You take care now." He did, eventually, head back to

the cruiser on the far side of the street, near where he had pointed for the sno-cone trailer.

Katie opened the door, clambered through to the back, grabbed Jaspurr, the harness and the leash and scrambled back outside, locking up and heading across The Green and past the central fountain, to the cookie shop.

Chapter 3

The Competition

KATIE WAS EXCITED TO CHECK OUT ROOKIE'S Cookies, owned by a man who had a very successful rookie year in the MLB before sustaining an ankle injury that benched him for good. With that dream ended before it had hardly started, he explored his other love — baking!

Jaspurr was wrapped up under her left arm when she timidly entered the shop. "Can I bring him in if I hold him? He's on a leash as well."

"Sure thing, as long as he's not sampling the merchandise. What's his name?"

Katie stepped in and let the door close behind her. There was no line, so she stepped up to the register, but not too close, examining the overhead menu board while answering. "Jaspurr, with 'urr' at the end like purr."

"Very nice. And, does Jaspurr like sweet treats?"

"I'm sure he would, but I don't let him have them. His treats tend to be fishy."

"Understood." He made a single, strong nod gesture. "And what about Jaspurr's owner? What's her name?"

"My name?" She had been thinking so hard about the cookie choices, she was caught off guard by the request for her name. "Ummm... Katie. I wasn't expecting that."

"No problem, Katie. What can I get for you?"

She looked at the list of flavors for Thursday, as every day had a different list. She wished she had made it in yesterday for the Mint Chocolate Chip. "I guess, since it's not Wednesday, I'll get Cookies and Cream. I have an ice cream truck on The Green for the next four days, so I'll stick to an ice cream flavor."

As he turned around to serve up the Cookies and Cream cookie, he asked, "What about Wednesday?"

"Oh, just that I would have loved to get the Mint Chocolate Chip, also an ice cream flavor."

He turned back to her with a wide grin. "It just so happens that I have some Bloopers from yesterday."

"Some what?" Katie wasn't sure she wanted any of that.

"They're the cookies that don't look as perfect or were from the day before. I sell them at half price, and I might have a Mint Chocolate Chip left."

Katie let out a big sigh of relief. "That's so much better than what I was thinking. Yes, I'll take one of those as well."

He added the second cookie to its own wrapper and handed both to Katie. "So, you've got an ice cream truck on The Green? What's that about?"

"I live in it. I gave up my apartment for a traveling life with Jaspurr, and I'm loving it."

"Well, you best be introducing yourself to the owners of Scoop of the Day. They have a similar schtick where their menu changes each day. They're only open Thursday through Sunday, so getting over there before the market might be a good idea."

"Out of curiosity, why should I introduce myself?"

"Let's just say, they're a little territorial. Not that I think they'd do anything to your truck, but it's worth preventing a negative interaction in front of customers."

"Really?"

Every town had an ice cream shop, it seemed, and Katie's truck was a novelty that came and went after a few days. She found it hard to believe she would really impact another business enough to cause a problem or prompt a reaction, even if it was only verbal.

"I'll deny it was me who said anything, but you don't deserve any guff from them while you're here such a short while."

"Thanks for the heads-up." Katie collected her two cookies then placed them back on the counter. "I haven't even paid you yet. My head's in the clouds today, trying to get into scooping mode."

"As long as you don't mention me, they're on the house."

She zipped her lips. "Nothing from me except thanks. Maybe I'll see you over at the truck. It's called *Where's the Scoop?*, you know, because I drive around."

"Oh, Mr. Frazellie is gonna *love* that," he said,

emphasizing the word love sarcastically. "It even has scoop in the name."

"So, how do I find Mr. Frazellie?"

"Scoop of the Day is down the next street like two blocks. You won't be able to miss the sign, but they might not be open yet for a Thursday. Good luck."

Katie picked her cookies back up and started for the door. "If this ends badly, I'm coming back here for my sympathy cookies on Sunday."

"Closed on Sunday, so make sure you need sympathy by Saturday at six." He winked.

"I didn't get your name." As Katie opened the door to leave, another customer was entering.

"Let's say it's Darron, just in case you feel the need to talk. If not, come back Saturday to find out what it really is, and maybe we'll go out to dinner."

"Have a great day, *Darron*," she hollered over her shoulder before the door closed, not giving him the time of day about whether or not his actual name was Darron.

Placing Jaspurr down on the ground to shake out his fur, Katie said, "Let's go meet this business owner."

She walked with purpose in the direction of Scoop of the Day, led by Jaspurr. After more than two blocks — Darron was no longer to be trusted — she could see the sign for her competition, though she didn't really see things that way. The open sign in the front window wasn't lit, but she could see someone entering through a side door. She hustled up to the shop, hoping to catch them before they disappeared.

"Excuse me. Excuse me!" She was still pretty far

away when she shouted, but it appeared they heard her on the second try. The figure in the doorway, carrying two large milk crates, stopped and looked at her. She picked up Jaspurr to run faster and hollered, "I'm coming."

"We're not open yet," the woman stated as Katie approached.

"I know, and I'm not looking to buy ice cream. I was hoping to speak with the owner." Katie made the assumption that this woman was too young to be the owner, and she hoped it didn't come back to bite her.

"Dad's not in yet." She entered the building and let the door slam shut.

Since Katie didn't know if she'd be coming back out, she checked out the exterior of the ice cream shop. The siding was a faded yellow with a bright blue awning that must have been replaced in the past few years. Cement steps led up to the ordering windows that sat beneath a massive menu of ice cream flavors and options. If Katie didn't feel intimidated by Darron's description of the owner, their business was certainly up to the task.

The door was pushed open again, startling Jaspurr in her arms. Katie scrambled to gain a better and safer hold on him as a formidable presence walked in her direction. She knew she hadn't done anything wrong, nor had she said why she was there, but the direct stare that seemed to go straight through her was intimidating.

"You were looking for me?"

"Mr. Frazellie, I presume. My name is Katie, and I wanted to introduce myself." She reached out her right hand below Jaspurr for a friendly handshake that wasn't returned. Once she wrapped the offending hand back around her cat, she said, "I have an ice cream truck on The Green for the weekend, starting tonight, and I just wanted to introduce myself before the market opened. I'm guessing we'll both be busy during the same hours, so I might not get another chance."

"Just like the city to go approving your truck when I'm having a hard enough time staying open. They're always looking out for themselves, not thinking about us little guys in the trenches."

"What little guys are you talking about?" she asked, sincerely.

"Me. My family. My business. The city just wants your money for permission to park and sell on The Green, but do they give two hoots about what your presence will do to my sales all weekend? No, they don't."

"I wouldn't worry too much about my little truck and Jaspurr." She scratched under his chin. "We're not going to do enough volume to keep up with you." Katie wanted to downplay the situation, but she knew her truck was a magnet for children and adults alike. Kids thought the idea of owning an ice cream truck was just as cool as Katie thought about it, and adults had great childhood memories of hearing the ice cream truck go by on a hot day in July.

"Your location and ability to move if you want to is something I can't compete with. When everyone goes to the market tonight, they'll see your ice cream truck."

"That is true. However, I'm only around for this one

weekend. I'll pack it up and move on Sunday night. No harm, no foul."

His look conveyed that her presence was both harm and foul to his livelihood. "Just stay in your lane. The police here don't take kindly to people breaking the rules."

Did he just threaten her? "I've already met one of your fine, upstanding officers, and he was absolutely professional and pleasant to work with."

"Let me guess, Officer Beauregard?"

"Huh. How did you know?"

Mr. Frazellie practically growled. "He's new here, that's how I know. Hasn't really figured out how we do things around here."

The woman Katie first spoke with exited the same door she had disappeared through. "Dad, I've got everything in the freezers. What else needs to be done?"

He waved his daughter over. "Jessie, this is Katie. She's got an ice cream truck over on The Green this weekend. If our profit is down, you can thank this woman."

"Dad, I just need to know if there's anything else I need to do before I go to Derek's house." Katie wasn't sure Jessie could have said anything more offensive to her father unless she opened a frozen yogurt store across the street.

"You're not going to Derek's house. You're working today, remember?" She huffed, stomped her foot and ran back to and through the side door. "Kids. Gotta learn the value of hard work."

Katie decided to keep her thoughts to herself. "I'll just get going back to my truck. Have a nice day. Nice to meet you, Mr. Frazellie." She put Jaspurr down and started walking, not waiting for a response — which never came.

When she got to her truck, tents were starting to pop up all over the fenced-in park locals called The Green. She placed Jaspurr in the loft bed space and attached the mesh barrier to keep him up there while the sales window was open. She had been able to leave the generator off while she went about town, but it was needed now before she started to open and close the freezers as ice creams were ordered. The tub of waffle cone mix was extracted from a small fridge where she had placed the two cookies from Rookie's Cookies with only one bite missing from each. She prepared a handful of cones ahead of time, but she knew she'd be making them on the fly all evening.

The farmers' market was a great event, even better than she had hoped for. The line was constant but manageable, and she was able to meet lots of local business owners who were curious about who she was and where she came from. The other food trucks were similarly busy the whole evening, and she felt good about not drawing away business from them. Having found herself working non-stop from before the market opened until after it officially closed, she missed out on all of the — what she suspected were— delicious offerings.

As she was wiping things down for the evening, a familiar face showed up. "Should I call you Darron?"

"Depends. Did you tell anyone we spoke?" He was trying to pull off being a secret spy, but it was coming off as more of an assistant soccer coach vibe.

"No one asked who sent me, so you're in the clear. What are you doing here?"

"I wasn't busy tonight, so I figured I'd check on you. Everything go well with Mr. Frazellie?"

She chuckled. "He wasn't happy about me and only vaguely threatened me, so I figure that's a win."

"Threatened you? How?"

"Nothing serious. He was madder that the city gave me a permit. Whatever. I hate to cut this short, but I need to get Jaspurr out for a walk and get some rest. I'll be here and open tomorrow at noon. Will I happen to see you tomorrow?"

"Not sure. Let's play it by ear. Good night, Katie." He walked off, into the darkness.

Katie would have loved to chat more, but she was exhausted. Taking a look around the truck, she closed up the rear door and locked it for the night with her inside. She grabbed Jaspurr out from the loft so he could relieve himself before bed, and they used the passenger door to get in and out. Once back inside, she didn't turn any lights on to make sure no one knew she was sleeping in there. With the privacy panels up, she should have gone undetected.

It was the middle of the night when she heard what sounded like two people arguing. She tried to go back to sleep, but it was impossible. There was no way to see what was happening outside the truck from the loft, so she descended the ladder and peeked through a slit between the edge of the driver's side door and the privacy panel. When she didn't see anyone, she climbed back into bed, counting cookies served up by Darron instead of counting sheep. Before drifting back off, she remembered she didn't confirm his real name and put that at the top of her to-do list for tomorrow along with finding out what all the fighting was about.

Chapter 4

The Discovery

It wasn't morning — Katie could tell by how tired she still was — but something told her to get up. She wiped her face with her hand and checked for the time. "Four. Why am I up again?" She took a quick assessment of her body. She didn't need to use the bathroom, though at this hour there wasn't one to use anyway. Her instincts said to get up, so she did. When she pulled back the privacy panel, red and blue lights filled the cab of the truck. Thinking quickly, she grabbed a baseball cap to cover her hair and pulled her arms through the sleeves of a light hoodie she had hanging on the back of the driver's seat. With flip flops always at the ready, she got out of the passenger side of the truck, hoping not to be noticed exiting. While she had permission to keep the truck parked there, and permission to sell ice cream, she was relatively confident she didn't have permission to be sleeping in the truck on The Green.

When she walked around to the other side of the

truck, she could see emergency personnel around the black fountain in the center of The Green. She approached, slowly, to find that the area had not been blocked off. Apparently, her casual demeanor gave her some kind of invisibility cloak because she was mere feet away from an unmoving body casually draped in the fountain before anyone said anything to her. The area was still quite dark as no emergency lighting had been set up on the scene.

"Ma'am. Excuse me, ma'am, you can't be here."

"I was just coming out to see what the fuss was about. You woke me up." She immediately regretted saying anything or even getting out of her truck because the polite police officer turned out to be Officer Beauregard.

"If it isn't Mrs. Ice Cream Truck. How was the market?" He moved to stand between her and the fountain with a body in it.

"Very profitable, thank you for asking. I'm just disappointed that you saw me with a wet mop of hair the last time and bedhead this time. Third time's a charm, I guess." She tried to peek over his shoulder to get a better look at the body. "When I said I might see you tonight, this is not what I meant."

Katie could see what she assumed to be a man, large in stature, lying on his back with his chin tilted up, but his head not fully submerged. Since she wasn't there first, she didn't know if the body had been found in that position or moved once discovered. The visible hand looked normal, not what she'd expect for a dead person, so maybe he hadn't been gone that long. He seemed to be wearing far too much clothing for a warm summer night, too much fabric. It appeared he had a jacket over at least one shirt, possibly with an undershirt, and pants with boots. She was so distracted by her own train of thought, she almost missed the officer asking her a question.

"Katie, we need you to leave. Where are you staying? Katie? Are you listening to me?"

"Yes, I'm sorry. I'll get on my way, but I had a window open earlier and heard two men arguing. Is that possibly important?"

"Do you know what time that might have been?"

"No clue. It woke me, which is why I think I wasn't sleeping well and woke again. I wouldn't even know how to attempt a guess because I didn't look at a clock."

"It might be important. When you woke up, did you see or hear anything else?" Officer Beauregard started to take notes on a small notepad and got lazy about blocking Katie. She pounced on the opportunity and walked past him and closer to the body.

Mr. Frazellie was sprawled in the water of the fountain with two large bumps on his head — one near the right temple and one at his hairline above his right eye.

"Ma'am, I'll need you to back up," Officer Beauregard announced once he saw she had moved.

"I know this man. I spoke with him before the market today. He was very upset that the town had approved my permit. Made a big deal about how the city only cared about collecting their money for the permit and not about small businesses that were already here. It was something like that."

"Clearly, we'll need to talk to you on a more official level based on what you're saying." He turned to the other officer on the scene. "Officer Fitch, this is Katie Thorne. We'll need to get an official statement from her in the morning." The second officer, a tall and fit young man, only grunted and lifted his chin.

"Do you just mean later this morning? And how do you know my name? I never told you." Katie put her hands on her hips, opening the front of the hoodie to reveal her pajama top. Nothing was improper about what she was wearing, but Officer Beauregard turned and shielded his face like a southern gentleman.

"I saw your permit and made a note of your name in case we crossed paths again," he said from behind his hand.

She wrapped the two sides of the zip-up hoodie around her body and crossed her arms. "Would you like me to go somewhere for this more formal statement?"

"Can you be at the station for nine? Will that be early enough for you to not miss business hours?"

She thought for a moment. I'll have to take the truck to do that. Do you have a big enough parking lot for me to turn around in or pull through? I mean, I'm capable of driving it, but I'm not stupid enough to get into an accident in a police station parking lot." She was the only one to laugh.

"How about I meet you?"

The idea that he was about to ask where she was staying needed to be prevented. "Let's just meet here so I

33

can get some things ready for the day in case it takes a while."

"Sure. I can drive you to the station so you don't need to move the truck. Would that dill your pickle?"

"I'd really appreciate that. Thank you." Katie was beginning to feel like a southern to northern translator might be in order.

"I'll see you here at nine. Go get some shut eye."

Katie turned away from the officer, the fountain and the body. Knowing she wasn't about to get any sleep, she climbed into the truck and set up a pen and pad of paper on the top of a freezer.

The two banks of freezers ran on either side of the truck, potentially allowing her to have windows open on both sides. As a solo business owner — other than Jaspurr's moral support — she hadn't found a reason to open the second window yet. Jaspurr, woken by the sound of the truck door, jumped down to sit on the freezer next to Katie.

"Jaspurr, here's what we know so far." He crouched down in the loaf position facing Katie, his eyes locked on her face. "There is a dead body, Mr. Frazellie, in the fountain in the center of The Green. Officer Beauregard and Officer Fitch are on duty, investigating the death. I have a meeting at nine where Officer Beauregard is going to pick me up here, at the truck. We'll need to make sure you're all set before that because I'm pretty sure they aren't going to let me bring you to the station for a visit."

He hadn't shown any orange-cat tendencies recently,

but she couldn't be sure how he would handle being alone for that long.

"Given the uncertainty of the situation, we should take a nice long walk before I go. Anyway, I want to talk to Darron, if that's his real name, about any conflicts Mr. Frazellie has had in the past — people who might want revenge or had a bone to pick. Maybe I should talk to his daughter, the one we met briefly. When we go for our walk, let's check who has a view of The Green. If I heard the arguing, maybe someone else heard it or saw something. I wonder if I'd be able to place the voices if I heard them again."

She thought about that while she smoothed Jaspurr's fur from head to tail. Would she be able to remember the voices she heard last night? She hadn't heard them for long, and one was probably Mr. Frazellie, but she hadn't noticed that at the time. Was it possible she was the worst witness in history? She had seen nothing, didn't know what time it was, nor did she recognize the voice of the deceased.

On the paper she wrote a list: Walk Jaspurr, talk to Darron, investigate around The Green, interview with Officer Beauregard, shower. When she wrote shower, she began to panic. Picking up her phone, she checked online for the times she would be able to get in to shower before Officer Beauregard was planning to pick her up.

"Jaspurr, let's go for that walk so I can check out who might have seen or heard anything. I need to be at the gym right at eight when they open to shower so I'm not gross for the interview."

Her feline friend jumped across the truck from one freezer to the other and attempted to paw his harness and leash down from the hook. Once it was on the floor, he slipped into it on his own, waiting for Katie to buckle the harness.

"You're so wonderful. This is why I don't need any other men in my life. Katie climbed up to the loft bed long enough to put on real clothes then hopped down to take Jaspurr for a walk.

The walk around The Green showed that the likelihood of someone else being able to hear or see a death in the middle of the night was slim. Obviously, the two restaurants were closed by the time she heard the argument, as was City Hall, and no one would have been at the bank or jewelry store in the middle of the night. While the Post Office may have had someone working in a sorting capacity, the likelihood they could be witnesses was slim. The library and other small businesses would probably have been unmanned at that time as well. The only real possibility Katie could think of was the former Hotel Rogers, now senior housing, on the opposite side of The Green from where she was parked.

Katie walked by the four-story structure twice, making sure to stay on the side of the road furthest from where the investigation was still underway. The front entrance appeared to have a patio area at ground level. No one was sitting there at the moment, but that didn't mean a night owl or insomniac wasn't there in the past few hours. She decided Jaspurr would need another walk after the interview, at which time she'd try to talk to anyone who might be willing and available, without needing to enter the building. Katie figured gossip traveled quickly in an apartment-style building like this, if the Pine Knoll Retirement Community was anything to go by.

With her morning plans sorted, she returned to the truck with Jaspurr, after making at pass by the gym to confirm the times she found online.

"Will you be a good boy while I go take a shower and visit the police station?"

Jaspurr walked over to his bowl and flipped it over with his nose then looked over his shoulder at Katie.

"Oh my, that won't do. I can't believe I haven't put food in your bowl since we've already been up so long." She grabbed the food bowl and turned it over, filling it with dry food for the day. She then grabbed a disposable bowl and filled it with wet food. While Jaspurr devoured the wet food, she washed out and refilled his water bowl, placing it on the opposite side of the truck from the food. "There. Now you should be all set.

Katie gathered what she would need for a shower and her minimal morning routine. Jaspurr used the top of the freezer to get into the loft bed, spinning in a circle two complete turns before settling into a curled-up sleeping position. With everything she needed in her shower bag, Katie took two steps up the ladder to give Jaspurr a few chin scratches, jumped down and exited the truck from the back.

The walk to the gym was uneventful, but she did notice a few people already relaxing on the patio in front of the senior housing building. The decision to shower instead of socializing was a difficult one, but needing to ride in a car with Officer Beauregard took precedent.

Katie was waiting outside the front doors of the gym with several other patrons when Ingrid showed up to let them in. She unlocked the doors from the inside, welcoming them for the morning.

"Oh, Katie. You're back. I didn't think I'd see you again. How long are you planning to stay today?"

Katie couldn't figure out her motive for asking, so she responded with the truth. "Just long enough to shower and look presentable for the day."

With a wink, Ingrid said, "Let's see if we can find you a complementary pass."

Chapter 5

The Station

"You are an angel." Katie knew she wasn't using all of the facilities, but she never asked for a handout. The way she had chosen to live her live — out of an ice cream truck with no plumbing — was exactly that, a choice. Money for gym visits was part of the plan, regardless of how much or how little she used them.

"Dear, this pass will be good until we close tonight, if you need to come back. I won't be here, but I approved it, so just keep track of this." Ingrid handed Katie a half-sheet of paper with the date and Ingrid's signature in purple marker.

"This is very kind of you. When you get out of work, stop by for an ice cream. My treat."

"You know, I just may take you up on that."

They shared a look of mutual respect as Katie hustled to the locker room. She was able to make herself presentable rather quickly this morning, knowing she needed to make it back to the truck before Officer Beauregard; she couldn't have him seeing her with the shower bag.

On the way out, Ingrid was busy helping someone with their membership pass, so Katie's exit was quick. She walked briskly to make the best time while not breaking into a sweat. Her hair was behaving this morning, and she didn't want to tuck it behind her ears this early.

When she got to the truck, Jaspurr, in true orange-cat fashion, had wedged himself under the privacy panels to sun his belly on the dash of the truck. While the scene may have concerned passersby, Katie knew Jaspurr always had a spot next to the freezers to cool down when necessary. She tapped on the glass when she got to it and scolded, "Little man, you should not be there." His response to her waggling finger was to lay his head back down from the response position to the tapping.

Katie entered the truck to organize and drop off the bag from the shower and check that her freezers were all organized, exactly the way she had left them the previous night. With everything stocked and as ready as it could be, she waited at a child-size picnic table near a small play structure for Officer Beauregard. His arrival at five minutes past nine was unexpected.

"Katie," he shouted from the open window of the cruiser. "Are you ready?" As she stood, he exited the car and opened the rear door. "Sorry about the ride." He offered her a hand to get into the back seat. She accepted and waited for them to start driving before asking her question.

"Do you really think this is necessary? I just don't think I'll be much help."

"The station is only about five minutes away, and we'll need a statement from you as a witness."

She couldn't figure out how she would get around the fact that in order to hear the fighting, she clearly had to have been in the truck. "Okay."

They spent the rest of the drive in silence, Katie taking in the uneventful drive to the station. Once there, she followed Officer Beauregard into the station and sat in a room with one metal table and three plain chairs.

"Officer Fitch is going to take notes and listen in." It wasn't a question, rather, a statement, that Katie had no opinion about. "Where were you last night when you said you heard an argument?"

"I was in the ice cream truck."

"In the middle of the night?" Clearly, he hadn't thought about her potential location before just now either.

"I fell asleep. It had been a long day of driving and walking and working. I just fell asleep in the passenger seat when I finally stopped to put up the privacy panels for the night."

"And why do you put them up?"

"I feel like someone is less likely to break in if they don't know for sure what's inside. What if I had a guard dog, or an alarm system? I know it's not much, but it's something."

Officer Beauregard looked over his shoulder to Officer Fitch. Once Fitch stopped scribbling on a small notepad, Officer Beauregard continued. "Can you tell us exactly what you heard and what woke you up the first time last night?"

"I heard two men yelling back and forth. I assumed it was an argument. It lasted a couple minutes before I went back to sleep. I lived in an apartment, back in my younger years, with so much noise outside all day and night, I learned to sleep through anything. Frankly, I'm surprised the argument woke me at all."

"You said it lasted a couple minutes. Did the argument stop or did you fall asleep when it was still going on?"

That was a good question. "I think it stopped, but I can't be sure. I was wondering about the voices mostly. I had spoken to Mr. Frazellie earlier, and I hadn't identified either voice as his, though one must have been."

"When did you speak with him and what did you speak about?" Officer Beauregard checked in on Officer Fitch again.

Katie couldn't tell this time if it was the same kind of check-in or they were communicating something different. "Sometime after noon because I already got cookies from Rookie's Cookies before heading down to meet Mr. Frazellie."

"You went to meet him on purpose? It wasn't just a chance meeting?"

"The man who owns and runs Rookie's Cookies..." she paused to see if she would finally get his real name.

"Darron."

"Yes, Darron. He told me it would be a good idea to

go introduce myself since I would be seen as a competitor. That it might be in my best interests to avoid any kind of confrontation during the market. I'm starting to think he may have been right."

Tilting his head to the side, Officer Beauregard asked, "Now, why would you say that?"

"He was plenty confrontational when I introduced myself. I'm glad he didn't go into a rant in front of customers or children, for that matter. I know I told you before, but he was upset at the city for giving me the permit."

"That's helpful information. I'll speak to the people at City Hall on Monday to see if they've had other confrontations with him. Can you speak more about Darron?"

"I went in to get a cookie, and I was the only customer. We talked about why I was in town, and he told me about maybe getting ahead of the explosion that is Mr. Frazellie."

Officer Beauregard looked like he was considering his next question carefully and hesitated.

"What is it?"

Rubbing his forehead, he asked, "Katie, I need to ask if you have an alibi for last night?"

"A what? Am I a suspect for something?"

"I can't turn a blind eye to the fact that you put yourself at the scene, hearing an argument you can't remember, with two voices you don't recognize. Do you have an alibi?"

She huffed and crossed her arms in front of her chest.

"I just got here. You know I don't live here. I have a cat. Does he count?"

"Unfortunately, he doesn't. I'd like to think it goes without saying, but we need you to stay in the area until we get this sorted. With that ice cream truck on The Green in summer, you'll be busier than a moth in a mitten this weekend."

She arched a brow in confusion. "Are we done here?"

Officer Beauregard let out a sigh. "I don't have any more questions for you at the moment. Officer Fitch, you got any?"

He looked up from his notepad, shook his head left to right and dropped his eyes back to the paper.

"Could you please take me back to my truck? You'll know where to find me if you have any more questions through Sunday."

"Why only through Sunday?"

"That's when my permission to park and sell there expires and I move on to another town."

He looked puzzled. "You'll need to make sure to contact us before you leave town if we haven't finished the investigation. We can't have you disappear without a permanent address. Is that fair?"

"I guess. Can we get going? I have things to do before I open the truck."

He stood and walked to the door, holding it open for her. They walked to the front of the building and exited, returning to his cruiser.

"Katie, you know this isn't personal. I'm new here,

and it's not been an easy start for me. To tell you the truth, I'm feeling as lost as last year's Easter egg."

She stifled a laugh. "I know I'm innocent and if you're checking, I have no motive. My truck did a great deal of business last night. I have nothing to gain from Mr. Frazellie's death. If you think about it, that's my alibi." She climbed into the waiting car, and Officer Beauregard closed the door behind her.

They traveled back to The Green in the same silence as they had arrived. She tried to open her own door, forgetting she was locked in the back of a police car. He opened her door for her once more and offered his hand to assist her climb out.

"Thank you." She accepted the gesture. "How did you end up in New Hampshire, anyway?"

He left the car running but shut both doors. "Well, I was having a run of bad luck and I saw an ad for police training where it was paid for if you did five years in the state you got certified, so I got on a bus up here. I didn't have a wife or kids tying me down, so this is where I landed. Not sure it's the right fit, but I'm gonna make it work for a while. I'm a by-the-book cop, so I'm not always the most popular 'round these parts."

"Mr. Frazellie had you pegged."

"As far as I was concerned, the man was as worthless as gum on a bootheel, but he had a family-owned business in town which I respected, even if we didn't have much respect for each other's personalities."

"Does that make you a suspect, Officer Beauregard?"

He smiled. "Unlike you, Ms. Thorne, I have an alibi.

Now, don't leave town." He tried to sound firm but broke his own stern look within a few seconds.

"Yes, sir." She attempted a salute that failed miserably. "Have a nice day." She walked around to the back of the truck and entered. With the rear door closed, she crept to the front and peeked through the gap between the privacy panel and the door frame to see if he had left.

Katie knew she hadn't done anything wrong. Heck, she was in the truck all night, right where she wasn't allowed to be. Two more nights of this sneaking around, and she'd move on to the next city or event she hadn't scheduled yet. Checking her phone, she saw it was past ten in the morning, not leaving her much time to get around to see Darron and Mr. Frazellie's daughter. She was worried about opening at noon like she had posted and not getting a chance to touch base with everyone who might have more information than the police were looking for.

After giving it a second thought, she wondered why she hadn't told them her hypothesis about the senior living building on The Green and how a resident there might have heard something. Did she want to solve this mystery like she had at the Pine Knoll Retirement Community? It was an internal struggle she'd need to address later in the day.

"Jaspurr. Jaspurr?" He poked his head over the loft bed where he had clearly been sleeping. "Let's go out to meet some nice new people."

Hopping down on the freezer, Jaspurr stretched out his front paws as far as they could reach, failing at his attempt to make biscuits. He strutted to the end of the metal lids and knocked a container of treats onto the floor of the truck.

"Oh, I see how it is." Katie grabbed the leash and harness along with her sling bag before making her way to the end of the truck, offering Jaspurr two treats from the container before sealing it back up and readying him for another quick trip around Lebanon.

Chapter 6

The Daughter

THIS WAS EITHER GOING TO BE QUICK AND EFFICIENT or a total bust — Katie mentally prepared herself for the latter. She left the truck with Jaspurr and headed toward the library in front of her, curving left after the short end of The Green, and checked out the patio in front of the senior living building. One man sat in a rocking chair, obviously sleeping with his head tipped back and mouth wide. Her plan to interview other potential witnesses would need to wait until more people were outside and awake.

She pressed on, knowing that Rookie's Cookies wasn't open yet, but hoped Darron might be able to see her through the windowfront and take pity on her. Once she was on The Mall, she pressed her nose to the glass and used her hands to help see into the shop. There wasn't so much as a fan blowing a napkin to make it look like this place would open soon. Speaking to Jaspurrr, she said, "Strike two." She laughed at her own joke.

The last person she hoped to talk to was Jessie, though she wasn't confident that conversation would get her anywhere. She took the walk, longer than two blocks, back to Scoop of the Day, crossing her fingers Jessie would be there on a Friday morning. Katie sat down at one of the tables for customers and waited while Jaspurr checked out the nearby grass. After fifteen minutes, Jessie exited the building.

"Hey, Jessie," Katie stood and hollered in an upbeat way, as if she was getting the attention of a friend. She toned it down when she continued. "I don't know if you remember me, but my name's Katie, and..."

"I remember. You have that truck Dad told me about."

Katie approached after picking up Jaspurr. "I'm so sorry to hear about your dad. Do you have any idea what happened?"

"Why would you care? You'll be gone by the end of the weekend."

"That's true, but I'm still human. I can't imagine what it's like to lose a parent like that."

"Like what?" Jessie stared at Katie with her eyebrows tight.

"So, have you spoken with a police officer?" Katie didn't know what she could or should tell Jessie.

"Officer Fitch came to tell me my father was found in the park last night, deceased. Is there more?"

Katie hesitated. "I didn't find your father, but I did end up at the scene because I woke up in the middle of the night to police lights and wandered into the park."

"What did you see?" Her question was a mixture of curiosity and fear.

The assumption Katie made was that Jessie was either in her senior year or had just graduated. This business was probably something she'd do every summer, but not enough to be her whole means of income. The shock of losing her dad was monumental, but nothing compared to how she'd feel if she knew it might have been murder.

"Mr. Frazellie was in the fountain when I got there. From what I saw, he had two contusions on his face."

"Like, from falling? Do you think he hit his head on something?"

"I'm going to tell it to you straight. I heard some arguing last night before I saw your dad. It was late, and I wasn't paying close attention, so I'm not sure one of the voices was his, but if we put two and two together, I'm going to assume he was fighting with someone last night before he died."

Jessie's eyes turned glassy, but no tear fell. "My dad could have an argument with a rock, so that's not a major development. Did you hear what they were fighting about?"

"No. I was half asleep."

"That's a disappointment. No offense, and I'm not upset with you, but it'd be nice to have more information. My dad arguing is pretty standard."

"I'm sorry about that. Can you think of anyone who might have had a big enough argument with him to kill him? Was he generally disliked?"

Katie thought back to Darron first telling her about

Mr. Frazellie and how she figured he was just blowing things out of proportion. How big could a reputation be that a warning was necessary to soften the blow about meeting the man?

"I'd say people had a healthy amount of fear when it came to my dad?"

"No offence intended on my part, but how much pull could the owner of an ice cream shop have in a city like this?" Katie had done her research. Lebanon wasn't a large city, but it wasn't rural either.

"Let's see, former school board member, former selectman, former firefighter. You name it, my dad probably did it."

"Why all former? What was he doing now besides Scoop of the Day?" Again, Katie assumed the place wouldn't earn enough three out of four seasons of the year to pay the bills.

"In the fall he does lawn care and leaf removal, then snow removal in the winter. In the spring, he helps people clean up their yards from the winter. It's mostly cash work."

"You didn't answer the question before. Did he have anybody who might want him dead?"

Jessie's eyes showed she was going through a list in her head. "Mostly conflicts that were over nothing. He was more bark than bite."

"Anything between him and Darron at Rookie's Cookies?"

"Why would you ask about him? That's oddly specific."

Katie sighed. "If I'm going to tell it to you straight, I might as well tell it all to you. Remember how I showed up yesterday to talk to your dad?"

"Of course. It was yesterday," she said like a sarcastic teenager.

"It was Darron who told me I should come talk to your dad before he found out about my truck through the grapevine. Said he was territorial and by introducing myself ahead of time, I might prevent a negative interaction in front of customers. So, did they have a beef?"

"They went to high school together. He played baseball with my dad. Dad took it personally that Darron got to go to college, play ball, get discovered and had a shot at the majors. Ever since he came back, they've been at each other's throats over every little thing possible." The look of confusion on Katie's face must have been substantial because Jessie clarified. "When dad was a selectman, Darron was looking to open his shop. Dad put up every inch of red tape to try to prevent it. Came home and told all us kids about things he did to make Darron's life difficult because he'd always had everything just handed to him."

"You have siblings?"

"Four, but they're all younger. I was from before Dad married my stepmother. I'm the only one old enough to work, and now it looks like I'll be taking over."

"Silver linings and all, you're lucky to have a family business to take over. I'm guessing you're, what, about eighteen?"

Jessie corrected her. "There is no silver lining here. I

was set to go to college next month, and now I'm stuck with this. My stepmother doesn't know anything about the businesses my dad runs. I'm always the one who works Saturdays and Sundays with him, so who do you think will take over his contracts? Who do you think will be responsible for supporting four siblings since her step-mother doesn't work and stays home with two of them? Me, that's who."

Katie could see she'd stuck her foot in her mouth. The assumption that the summer business would become Jessie's and be a source of income and something to do when she wasn't in school was clearly the wrong impression.

"I'm so sorry. I made an assumption about the ice cream business and didn't think about the others. Can't you just not take those contracts over? People will find other businesses to clean their yard."

Jessie broke down in tears. With Jaspurr in one arm, Katie held Jessie's elbow with the other and walked her to a table. They sat together, and Katie waited for Jessie to take the time she needed to regain her composure.

"You don't understand. Without me, Stephanie won't be able to pay the mortgage or feed the kids. They're my brothers and sisters. I can't let them starve or be taken by the state. There's no insurance. There's car payments. I have to be the one to step up."

"Stephanie's your stepmother?"

"Uh huh." She wiped her nose with a napkin from her pocket.

"Why can't Stephanie sell the businesses? You go to

college, and she figures out how to continue raising the kids, but money from selling the businesses could buy her time."

After a few sniffles, Jessie responded, "I guess that's a possibility."

Jaspurr wriggled free of Katie's arms and walked across the table to give Jessie a headbump on her chin. He then jumped onto her lap and nuzzled her arm.

"Hey, sweetie. Thanks for that."

"I don't want to keep you any longer because I know you have a lot to do to get this place ready for a busy Friday, but the townspeople would understand if you didn't open." Katie looked up to see a perfectly blue sky with no clouds. "Finish out the season maybe, then consider selling, unless you wanted to keep this business in the family. There are a lot of decisions to be made, but none need to be made today."

"I appreciate you checking on me."

"Was there anyone else besides Darron that your dad had significant disagreements with?"

"The city. Anyone who worked at City Hall was a target for his wrath. I'm sure they won't be sad that he's gone."

"It sounds like your dad served this city well for some time. Even if they don't mind the conflict being gone, I'm sure they knew he was a good member of the community."

"If they're open, check with Jonah. That's who he usually fought with."

Katie perked up. "I met Jonah, well, talked to him on

the phone. That's who I originally set up my permit with. I'll see if I can get there today. Thanks."

"I'm going to get back to work. The shop won't run itself."

The two women stood after Jaspurr jumped down. "Want a hug?"

Jessie stepped toward Katie, both giving and accepting a hug.

"See you around."

Jessie headed back into Scoop of the Day, and Katie headed in the direction of The Green.

"Now, do we take our chances, Jaspurr, that Darron might be baking, or do we head straight for the patio?"

Jaspurr stopped walking and used his head to pull on the leash twice in quick succession.

"The second option? Sounds good."

Getting to the retirement home was practically the same direction as getting to the truck, so they stopped off at the truck first for two reasons. First, Katie wanted to change her hours of operation sign to show one as the opening time. If anyone had seen noon before, they might just think it was a mistake, at least that's what she hoped. The second reason was to see if Jaspurr wanted to stay in the truck. It had already been quite the walk for a small cat, and he might want some beauty sleep.

"Jaspurr, you can stay here if you want." She opened the back door, placed Jaspurr on the floor and waited. He rubbed his side up against a freezer, pulling at the harness. "I'll take it off so you can nap. I don't plan to be gone long, okay?" She removed the harness and hung it up with the leash. After a chin scratch, Jaspurr launched himself up onto the freezer then the loft bed and curled up.

Katie looked around, not needing to do anything else in the truck, then shut the door and headed off in the direction of the patio. She hoped someone else was a night owl and might have heard the argument. This time, she walked through the middle of the park, passing the fountain that was no longer considered a crime scene. She admired the fountain for a moment, knowing that most people would never associate it with a death the way she would. Next week when the farmers' market happened, it might not even be mentioned. At least, she hoped that was the case.

As she continued across the park, she noticed four people sitting in chairs on the patio of the senior living property. It seemed her luck had turned around. Now, she had to hope they were willing to talk.

Chapter 7

The Gang

Katie stepped onto the patio with three men in rocking chairs and one in a wheelchair. From the sidewalk, Katie learned the four were having a lively conversation about how one of them met a famous rock star when he was younger, and the other four didn't believe him.

"I did. He offered me a smoke, which I turned down, and wished me a good evening. Very nice gentleman," said the man at the far right of the patio as Katie looked on from the sidewalk.

"That's how we know you're not telling the truth," shouted the one closest to the entrance of the imposing brick structure. The two other men joined in the raucous laughter generated by the response.

"Hey, guys. I was wondering if I could break up this party for a minute or two?" Katie started to make herself small then straightened. She didn't want them to assume she was meek when she never had been before.

"Young lady, what can we do for you today?" asked the man who was telling the story.

"My name is Katie." She waited.

The storyteller stood, slowly. "My apologies. I'm John, this is Daniel, next is Joseph and the loudmouth is Frank." John shook her hand as Daniel and Frank stood to do the same. Katie then moved in front of Joseph to shake his hand as well.

"I'd stand, but I can't." He laughed, which put Katie at ease.

"Well, my questions have nothing to do with standing, so I guess we're all set."

"Would you like a seat, young... Katie," offered Frank. He changed his tune as soon as she looked at him.

"I'd love one. Thank you."

Frank walked to the opposite side of the entrance where there was a matching patio and grabbed one of the chairs, not a rocker, for Katie to use. When he placed it next to his rocker, he sat, offering her the seat he previously occupied.

"I'm fine with that chair. You don't need to give up yours."

"My mother would have my hide if I didn't offer you the better chair. Please, sit."

She did as instructed. "Last night, there was a dead body found in the middle of the park. Did you already know about it?" She was asking the group, waiting to see if someone responded stronger than the rest.

"We heard about it from one of the walking groups this morning," answered Joseph. "There's a group of women that go out walking together at the same time, and one of them has a scanner. Can't get anything past her."

"What did she tell you?"

"Vanessa told us just what you said. There was a call for more officers to respond to The Green for a suspicious death. No other details, but I'm guessing you have some."

Katie could feel her cheeks turn rosy. "Why would you assume that?"

Frank spoke up. "Never seen you round these parts before, but suddenly you want to talk to four old geezers about a death. Something's not adding up."

She felt like playing at least one of her cards now was appropriate. "Well, I came across two officers last night who were on the scene with a dead body in the fountain. I approached and got right up to them before they saw me, and that's when I identified the deceased."

This time it was Daniel who leaned in to participate. "Where did you say you were from, and why are you here?"

"Let's not get bogged down with that, just now. Let her tell us what she saw," demanded Frank.

"No." Daniel stood his ground with his friend. "Who are you, Katie?"

She cleared her throat, not expecting to be the one grilled. "I'm Katie Thorne, and I'm the one who operates that ice cream truck on the other side of the park. I drive around to different cities and towns, setting up my business for one or several days, and then I move on. I met the deceased Thursday morning before opening my truck.

Since I sell ice cream, I was advised to introduce myself to Mr. Frazellie."

"That was your first mistake. Ain't no one in town who likes him," confessed Joseph.

"Well, no one needs to worry about if they like him because he's dead. His body was laying in the fountain when I got up to the two officers, and he had two marks on his face. Know anyone who might have wanted to do him harm?"

Behind his hand, Frank joked, "Half the city." The other three men had the decency to not laugh.

"Why is his death funny to you, Frank?"

"Look, it's not funny, but Walter didn't have any friends that I knew of."

"Walter?"

"Walter Frazellie. The owner of Scoop of the Day. That's who we're talking about, right?"

Katie shook off the confusion. "Yes. I just hadn't heard anyone use his first name since I got here. I was starting to think maybe he didn't have one."

"He would be very happy to know you only knew of him as Mr. Frazellie."

"So, anyone make the short list of people who might want Walter dead?"

The men looked at each other, no one speaking.

Katie summed up what she believed to be true. "Everyone hated him, but no one wanted him dead. Interesting dynamic. Was it just an unlikable personality that turned people off, not actual actions?"

Daniel responded this time. "Hit the nail on the head."

"I guess that brings me to my next question. Any of you, or friends of yours, light sleepers or insomniacs? It would probably need to be someone with a room facing the street."

John, who had remained quiet, raised his hand like he was in school. "I am, and I do. Why?"

Katie turned her body and her attention fully to John who seemed to be the quietest of the bunch. "Before I ended up in the park, I heard an argument. It was two men, but either I didn't hear what they were saying or I forgot because I was woken unexpectedly. I was hoping maybe someone in this building might have heard something."

"I did hear an argument last night, but I wasn't paying attention either. Because my room faces the street, I often hear stuff in the middle of the night. It was a nice night, and I had my window open. I wish I had something for you, but I don't."

"Too bad. I figured maybe the people arguing were Mr. Frazellie and his killer. I went with the police to give a statement, and I felt like I didn't have much. Any chance anyone else could have heard anything?

"I can ask around the building. The people who don't sleep well all know each other. Want me to stop by again later?" John asked.

"I'll do you one better. If the four of you can ask around then stop by my ice cream truck, I'll treat you all to an ice cream."

Joseph rolled his wheelchair forward to get closer to Katie. "I think I speak for the gang when I promise you, we'll see you later, even if we don't have any new information."

"If you stop by, I'll give you the ice cream even if you don't come up with anything." She checked the clock on her phone. "Oh, I've got to get going. I planned to open at noon but I wanted to chat with you before, and now I've gone and made myself late."

"Don't you own the truck?" asked Frank.

"Of course I do. Why do you ask?"

"I mean, you make your own schedule, right?"

"Yes."

"How can you be late?"

She smiled. "I guess I'm not late, but I put up a sign for my hours. I'd hate to disappoint anyone, especially children. Katie stood and began to thank them for answering her questions when Daniel had one more for her.

"How was it that you heard the argument and ended up in the park last night? Where are you staying?"

"Can you keep a secret?"

"We might be part of the largest gossip train in the city, but we know when to keep our mouths shut. What gives?" Now Daniel was right in the thick of things.

"My truck has a loft bed. I live out of it with my cat, Jaspurr. I'm sure I'm not supposed to be staying in the truck when it's parked there in the spots for food trucks, but I don't have anywhere else. Don't tell the police or City Hall."

"You don't have to worry about us, but now we'll be worrying about you. Is it safe?"

She knocked on one of the rockers. "No problems yet. This time, I woke up to the argument. It's rare because I'm a pretty deep sleeper. Once that woke me, I'm guessing I never got fully back to sleep, that's why I was hoping you guys heard it as well. If it was the person arguing with Mr. Frazellie that killed him, a voice match would be great evidence."

Three of the men were standing now, and Joseph was already directly in front of Katie. They wished her good luck selling and promised to see her again that evening.

"It was nice to meet you all, and I look forward to hearing how successful the gossip train is."

She left, heading in the direction of Rookie's Cookies. However, she had to pass by City Hall to get there. She was torn. Should she get to the truck as quickly as possible, try to talk to someone at City Hall before they closed, or try to get to Darron before his place got busy. After a quick check of her phone, she noticed the window for talking to anyone at City Hall was closed because they didn't open again until Monday. Decision made, she started walking toward Rookie's Cookies.

When she got there, the place was already mobbed. There was no way she would get to talk to Darron in any substantial way. She grabbed a pen off the counter and a napkin to write him a note. Her name, phone number and time were jotted down and handed across the counter to him when he got close.

"I can't talk now," he started to say and got distracted.

"Darron, meet me at the truck tonight."

As he was walking away from her to respond to something beeping, he hollered, "Okay."

She took that as her sign to leave. Walking the remaining trip around the park got her back to her ice cream truck and Jaspurr. There was no one waiting in front of the closed window, so she breathed a sigh of relief.

The sight of Jaspurr when she had been out of the truck for a while always settled her mind. She knew he was perfectly fine taking long naps, as most cats do, but the idea that he might get into orange-cat mode and destroy the place did cross her mind. One time, he managed to get all of the plastic spoons out of their containers, tossing them all over the truck. He appeared to have had a grand time and slept well that night, but it was a chore to pick them up and expensive to replace.

When she got to the front cab, she found Jaspurr curled up in the passenger seat. He perked up and nuzzled her face when she got close enough. "Did you miss me?" she asked. He stood, stretched and put his two front paws on her shoulders in — what Katie pretended was — a hug position. "I missed you too. Let's get some fresh water in the bowl and write up the sandwich board for today."

She did both of those things, adding some new flavors that she transferred from a different freezer and removing ones that didn't sell well the previous day. With the generator running, she opened the window for sales.

Friday was always a good day for people to buy ice

cream, but not typically until after the workday ended. She saw several kids and moms with babies, but the volume really picked up after five. Of course, that was exactly when the four members of the gossip train showed up to collect their ice creams.

"Katie," Frank started, Joseph, Daniel and John right behind him, "we've got a word."

Chapter 8

The Possibilities

"CLIFF?" KATIE REPEATED BACK TO JOHN.

"That's what she heard, cliff."

"What who heard?" asked Katie.

Joseph rolled to the front of the group and explained, "I talked to everyone on the first and second floors with John. There's this one woman who really keeps to herself, Myrtle, and she woke to the sounds of the argument as well. She lives on the second floor. No one on the first floor sleeps with their windows open because it's a safety issue. Anyway, she also said she heard what sounded like two male voices arguing, and distinctly heard one of them say something about a cliff."

"Are there any significant cliffs in the immediate area?"

Joseph shrugged. "Nothing comes to mind, but we figured it was still something."

"Well, a deal's a deal. Which flavors can I get for you fellas? Tonight, we have Cookies & Cream of the Crop,

Chocolate Mudslide, Granite Toffee Crunch, Mint Chocolate Chip off the Old Block, Strawberry Fields Forever, Snickerdoodle, Everything But the Kitchen Sink and Very Vanilla.

In a not-so-surprising move, Frank ordered first. "I'm going with Strawberry Fields Forever, for my favorite music group. Can I get that in a plain cone, please?"

"Coming right up." She started to scoop Frank's order. "Joseph, what about you?"

"Dish of Snickerdoodle, please. I assume it's cinnamon flavored."

"You assume correctly. Cone or dish?"

"Sugar cone, please."

Handing Frank his plain cone of Strawberry, she asked Daniel next. "How about for you?" She bent to scoop Joseph's Snickerdoodle.

"Could I please get the Granite Toffee Crunch? In a dish, please."

"You guys are making this too easy." She handed Joseph's to Daniel. "Please pass that over."

Daniel's toffee was also an easy scoop. "John, what'll you have?"

John looked at the list of flavors on the chalk board like he hadn't had enough time yet. "Chocolate mudslide. Gotta stick with an oldie but goodie."

"I spoke too soon."

"How so?" asked John.

"I said you guys were making it too easy, but chocolate ice cream is always the hardest to scoop. It's the firmest flavor when frozen." She handed the Granite

Toffee Crunch to Daniel with a spoon. "Dish too?" she asked John, and he nodded. "Here goes nothing." She grunted and groaned while scooping this one, making a show of it. "If your ice cream is smaller, John, you'll know why." She was kidding, but scooping the chocolate was no joke.

With all four men sufficiently compensated for their efforts and information, Katie said good night to them. She still had a line of people to scoop for, and she wasn't about to turn someone away just because it was getting late.

She hadn't looked at a clock in a long time, but the appearance of Darron told her it was at least eight because that's what she wrote in her note. With no official closing time, she finished the last two customers in line and hollered out to Darron she'd come out in a few minutes, quickly closing the window so no one new lined up.

When she exited the rear of the truck, she had Jaspurr harnessed and leashed. "Couldn't leave him in there any longer," she confessed. "Can we go for a walk?"

Darron bowed his head. "As you wish."

"Nice reference. Trying to win me over?"

"With the Princess Bride reference, no. With this..." He handed her a box from his cookie shop. "I was hoping to win at least brownie points."

"Oh, what flavors did you bring me?"

"Banana Cream and Salted Pretzel. I took a guess."

Katie opened the box, took one cookie out and put the box with the second cookie in the truck, closing the rear door. She placed Jaspurr down on the sidewalk and started on the Banana Cream cookie.

"What did you want to talk to me about tonight?"

She swallowed. "What have you heard since we spoke last?"

"Well, when you own a shop with the traffic I have, you hear a lot. Figuring out what's true is a different beast."

"Start at the beginning, and I'll do my best to clear things up." She took another bite, appreciating the layers of flavor between the cookie and the topping.

"I was told that Mr. Frazellie was found dead in the park last night. I'm not sure what order I learned everything, but I heard that it was murder, then I also heard a drowning, and last I heard who it was."

"Any idea how you learned the identity? His next of kin didn't know until this morning, and I wouldn't expect she'd be telling everyone."

Darron paused both speaking and walking. After he started to move again, he spoke. "I'm pretty sure it came from someone close to his wife. She must have reached out for support when she found out. Terrible him leaving behind so many young children, and now Stephanie is going to be raising them as a widow."

"And Jessie. He's leaving behind Jessie as well."

"Of course, Jessie. I suppose she'll take over Scoop of the Day."

"Funny you should bring that up. She wants to head off to college but feels she has an obligation to take care of her family and run the businesses Mr.

Frazellie had. She also told me why her dad didn't like you much."

"No love lost there, but I didn't want him dead, if you're probing for clarification."

"According to Mr. Frazellie, he felt there were years of you getting things handed to you. He seemed to feel it was his job to put up roadblocks according to his own moral compass. Did you ever feel that way when you were trying to open Rookie's Cookies?"

"Absolutely. Every corner I turned there was another hoop to jump through or another little-known statute I was *maybe* breaking, so everything took longer and cost more than projected. I didn't realize until much later he was the one causing all the disruptions. We fought like cats and dogs on most occasions we crossed paths. I stayed away from his shop, and he stayed out of mine."

Katie figured she needed to see if the arguing might have also happened last night. "When did you see him last?"

"Geeze." He rubbed his forehead. "Months probably. I think there was a town meeting we were both at, but we didn't speak to each other. Couple dirty looks, maybe." He chuckled at the memory.

"Well, something you don't know is that I was on the scene after his body was found. I heard an argument between two men, and later woke to the police around the fountain in the center of the park. I walked right up to them and saw his body lying in the fountain."

"Katie, I'm so sorry you had to see that. Why were

you up in the middle of the night, and how did you hear the argument?" His look of concern seemed sincere.

Katie figured if she was going to lie about something once, she should probably keep the lie consistent. "I fell asleep in the truck. I was so tired from the market, I passed out in the driver's seat. The arguing woke me, but I didn't really catch anything. I did, however, speak to a nice group of gentlemen on the other side of the green. One of them was also up and heard the argument, so I know I wasn't hallucinating."

"So, the thought is whoever was arguing was probably Mr. Frazellie and his killer? What if he wasn't killed? What if it was an accident. Drunk. Tripped. Face in the fountain. Is that possible?"

"He had two marks on his face that looked like he was struck by something, so I don't think he just tripped and fell, though I suppose it's possible. It'd also be a pretty big coincidence to hear the arguing before he turns up dead and for them to not be connected, don't you think?"

"I do. Even though you didn't hear what was being said, did you recognize the voices?" Katie wanted to know if he was asking because he was one of the voices, but she wasn't brazen enough to go there just yet.

"Wouldn't it be pretty shocking if I did? How long have I been here? If you and Mr. Frazellie got into a fight, maybe I'd recognize your voices, but it was the middle of the night. I wasn't really awake. I feel responsible for not having more information."

Darron turned and held Katie's shoulders at arm's

length. "Do not beat yourself up for that. I'm glad it wasn't me and you don't think it was my voice, but the odds of you knowing who it was are astronomically low. Heck, who shows up in a new town and solves a murder after a day or two?"

"You'd be surprised," she said under her breath. Back at full volume, she asked, "Can you think of any steep hillsides or drop-offs in the area? Anywhere that people might have a pattern of 'accidents' that aren't really accidents?"

"Are you looking to get rid of someone? Maybe, push someone off the edge, never to be heard from again?" He gave her a cautious smile.

"Just thinking through a number of possibilities, and no, I'm not looking to take any lives."

At this point, Katie and Darron had made two complete laps around The Green and were now back at the ice cream truck, Jaspurr sitting at Katie's feet.

"I'll leave you to get this place all wrapped up for the night. I'm sure there's a lot of cleaning to do. If you want to talk more tomorrow, I'll be in the shop before noon. Just knock on the window."

"Actually, before I start cleaning, do you know who Mr. Frazellie was mad at what he said the city didn't care about his business?"

"Maybe a city clerk or the city manager. Not really something I know much about. Why? Thinking that could be someone who wanted him dead?"

"I just don't know. As an outsider, it seems like there were a lot of people he rubbed the wrong way and didn't like him, but I just can't find anything worth killing him over."

"As a local, I'd agree with the summation."

Katie opened the back of the truck and let Jaspurr in, unhooking his harness. She closed the door but didn't latch it. "You brought me cookies. Can I send you off with an ice cream?"

"I thought you'd never ask."

She recited the available flavors, and he picked Snickerdoodle, just like Joseph had. "Is this on your list of cookies currently?"

"Tuesdays right now, but it's not always in the rotation. People really love that my snickerdoodle has frosting on top."

"Cone or dish?"

"You don't have a waffle cone back there, do you?"

"I'll see what I can do." She winked and disappeared inside the truck. When she reappeared, she had a waffle cone with two scoops of a vanilla base with swirls of cinnamon and sugar throughout. "Here you go."

"This looks delicious. I hope you have a nice rest of your night, after cleaning, of course."

"Of course. Maybe I'll see you tomorrow."

Darron waved as he walked away, presumably toward wherever he parked his car during business hours. Katie climbed back into the truck and onto the loft bed with Jaspurr.

"Jaspurr, how am I going to talk to someone from the city if the office is closed? It'll look weird if I start calling people at home or messaging them on social media. I've talked to everyone else I thought was important. Jessie is in a tough spot with a lot of important decisions to be made. Darron seems to be at peace with the conflicts he and Mr. Frazellie have had over the years. Even the guys at the retirement home had the same message — no one liked him, but killing him was too much. There must be something we don't know about Walter."

Katie did a quick search online and found that city records and newspaper articles are also held at city hall, so there would be no way for her to access them until Monday.

"Drat."

Suddenly, she jumped off the bed and onto the ladder. Taking just one rung to assist her descent, she leapt into the front seat and removed the privacy panel. The paperwork giving her permission to park and sell had a phone number on it in case of emergencies along with the name of the contact person, Linda. Katie had already met Linda when getting her paperwork settled for this visit to Lebanon, and tomorrow morning, she'd be calling her up to see if there was anything else she could do to help Katie solve this murder.

Chapter 9

The Clerk

KATIE HAD A TOUGH TIME FALLING ASLEEP. THOUGH she was clearly exhausted, the paths her brain went down were nothing short of a labyrinth. Would she start in the library looking for newspaper articles or start by calling Linda? Were Jessie, Darron and 'The Gang' all tapped out as resources, or were two of them possible suspects? Eventually, she passed out with Jaspurr on the pillow beside her head.

The next morning, she was woken by a rough tongue to the face. "Okay, okay. I'm up." Checking the phone, she realized it was ten. She had slept much later than usual, which is probably why Jaspurr's stomach or bladder was telling Katie to start her day. She got up and put on a baseball cap, the best she had to offer — at least it was a Red Sox cap, and Lebanon was still fully in the zone for that. By the time she was dressed, Jaspurr was sitting with his harness and leash at the back door of the truck.

They went for a walk along side streets this morning, not the same walk around The Green they did twice last night with Darron. When Jaspurr started to slow down, Katie took him back to the truck. She checked again in the small mirror she had posted in her sleeping area. "As good as I'm going to get," she told Jaspurr, now lying on the bed. "No one really cares what you look like scooping ice cream, do they?" With no reply, she called the emergency number for Linda.

After half a ring, she answered, "Linda here. How can I help you?"

"Linda, it's Katie, with the ice cream truck."

"Ahhh, Katie. Everything going okay?"

She pulled a face Linda couldn't see through the phone. "I suppose so. Look, I'm only here for one more day, and I was hoping to learn more about the city. Any chance you are at City Hall today working on your day off?"

"That obvious?"

"Well, those of us who love our work don't treat it like work." She was laying it on thick.

"If you wanted to come down, I'm probably here another hour."

"You are amazing. I'll be right over. Give me five minutes. Thank you." Katie was so excited she ended the call before allowing Linda to respond. "Jaspurr, I've changed the water and there's new dry food. I'll be back as quickly as possible." With her bag over her shoulder, she dashed out the back of the truck and locked up.

Arriving at City Hall — literally across the park from

where she was parked — meant crossing paths with the fountain Mr. Frazellie had died at. She had a determined pep in her step to figure out what happened to him.

As Linda had suggested, she called the number again when she got to the door to be let in.

"Come on in, hunny."

Katie entered through both sets of doors while Linda locked them behind her. "I can't thank you enough. When I come to a new town, I like to learn about it. My initial plan was to stop in yesterday, but I found out too late that you were closed on Fridays."

"I know. People who've lived here twenty years still don't look at the hours of operation, so you're one up on them. This way."

Linda escorted Katie to the room with both paper and digital files. "As long as you're not planning to steal anything, you've got about an hour." She booted up an ancient computer and logged in. "Here's where you can search online, and if we have a paper version of anything it'll have a reference number assigned to the digital file. Knock yourself out."

"Thanks again." Linda exited. Jokingly, she said to herself, "If I hadn't heard two men arguing, I'd be wondering if it wasn't Linda who knocked Mr. Frazellie out." That made Katie think again. She ran out into the hallway after Linda. "Hey, any chance you know someone who might have wanted to harm Mr. Frazellie, the man who owns Scoop of the Day?"

"Too many to count, hunny. Why?"

"Haven't you heard? He was found dead in the middle of the night, early Friday morning."

"I guess I do work too much. I hadn't heard, though I'm not really in a position to hear rumors. Has it been on the news? Never mind, doesn't matter. What happened?"

"Well, that's what I'm trying to figure out. I wanted to look back at any meetings he had as a selectman or meetings where he was against something the city was planning. If I use the digital files, can I search his name?"

Linda was still flustered by the news and waved her hand to cool her face. "Yes, that should work, if he said something on record, but you'll have your work cut out for you."

"Why do you say that?"

"He had an opinion about everything this city did or proposed, and he didn't keep it to himself."

"Best I get started."

For the next hour, Katie searched for Mr. Frazellie and Walter Frazellie, writing down conflicts, motions and proposals as well as the other people involved in each, whether an individual or a company. She wrote the list out after having to go ask Linda for paper and a pen. The list took on a life of its own, and Katie wished she had a laptop to sort the data.

When an hour had gone by, she checked with Linda who gave her another thirty minutes. Right back at it, Katie searched through over five years of records, again coming up with no one who might obviously want him dead.

"Linda," she said, entering her office, "I need

someone to look at my list and see if there are any connections I'm not seeing. How long have you lived in the city?"

"Hunny, I've lived here my whole life and done this job for almost forty years. Let's look at your list together."

They discussed possible connections, family and business relationships, and Katie asked about one hundred questions. At the end of it, she had found nothing of significance.

"Linda, what about Mr. Frazellie's relationships? He had Jessie with someone other than Stephanie. Who was that?"

"Jessie's mother was the love of his life. Her name was Camille. They were high school sweethearts and had Jessie shortly after they were married. When Jessie was maybe two years old, Camille disappeared."

"Do you think he killed her?" Clearly, Katie had been thinking about this case far too much to jump straight to that conclusion.

"No one knows why, and he never said, but she told him she was leaving, and she did. Camille was never heard from again. Rumors swirled about her heading out to California to sing or traveling up to Canada to escape from an unknown crime. Whatever it was, she abandoned poor Jessie with her young father. That's how he ended up with so many random jobs around town."

"Clearly, we can't ask him, and Jessie wouldn't know. It'll forever be a mystery, but that's helpful extra information. Before I leave, I've got one more question, and it's going to come out of left field. Are you ready?"

"You've already thrown every curve ball today, so why not another."

"Is there anywhere really steep in the area where people jump off or happen to fall off by accident? Do you have many fall-to-their-death incidents in the area?"

"I mean, Quechee Gorge isn't too far, but I can't imagine anyone would call that local. It would qualify as part of the Upper Valley, I suppose, but not really local. There's a bridge with sidewalks across it, and the view is incredible. There have been people who've taken their own lives before, so they've put up fencing to prevent it. Why?"

"Just another wild hypothesis I'm testing out, and it's coming up empty."

"Does it have anything to do with Jessie's mother? They searched there when she disappeared, but they found nothing."

Katie shuddered. "No, nothing to do with her. I'm sure Jessie would love some closure now that she'd lost both parents, but I fear that isn't in the cards. Thanks for your help, Linda."

"I'm just sorry we didn't find the connection you were looking for."

"That's okay, and I appreciate your help. I'm going to take this to the police and see what they can do with it. It's funny, you know, that I was knee-deep in this death investigation before I ever learned Mr. Frazellie's first name. On the paper where I took the notes, could you fill in a few blanks for me before I take this to the police. They have so much to do, I figure this is a kind of public service and right up both our alleys." Katie tried to look cute and innocent to entice Linda into giving up more of her personal time to help.

"No problem, hunny. Hand the list back, and I'll do my best."

Fifteen minutes later, Katie walked out of City Hall with at least ten pages of handwritten notes in a nine-by-twelve clasp envelope to turn over to Officer Beauregard when they got to the police department.

The walk back to the ice cream truck was almost chilly. Clouds were rolling in and a strong breeze had developed while she was in City Hall. Opening the ice cream truck late today, if at all, didn't seem like it would be a problem. She walked back through the center of the park, silently apologizing to Mr. Frazellie as she passed the fountain. She really thought after the mysterious death in Maine where she helped find the killer this would be a piece of cake — or a scoop of ice cream.

After calling the number on the card provided the night of the death, Katie checked on Jaspurr then waited on a picnic table for Officer Beauregard to come pick her up. When he arrived, he parked and got out of the car, locking it on his way over. She noticed, however, that a second cruiser also pulled up, but no one got out.

"Now, what do you have for me today?" he asked with a swagger before leaning his backside on the table.

"I have some information that I've collected, but I wanted you to bring me to the police department again for an official statement. If this isn't wrapped up by the time I leave tomorrow, I want to make sure you know everything I know before I go."

"Well, it's too bad that's not the only reason I'm here to pick you up."

"What could you possibly mean by that?"

Officer Beauregard straightened and took a pair of handcuffs from his uniform belt. "Katie Thorne, you are under arrest for the murder of Walter Frazellie."

"You have got to be kidding me. I called you to turn over the evidence I've collected for potential suspects, and you think I did it? I've been here, what, like fifty hours? Do you think Walter Frazellie is capable of getting me to murder him that quickly when he's been here his whole life making enemies? Wow, you're giving him a lot of credit and me none."

"Are you going willingly, or do I need to put the cuffs on?"

"I'm happy to go with you, since I didn't do anything and you have no evidence I was with him before his death. And let's not forget there are two other people who heard the same argument between two men I heard. Nah, let's get this party started." She stood and walked to his cruiser, waiting at the back door for him to open it.

"Don't forget to finish reading me my rights when we get back to the station before you start questioning me. I want everything to be on the record. Oh, and I'll need this envelope with me while we're having our little chat."

Katie climbed into the back once the door was open. Officer Beauregard closed her door then got into the driver's seat. According to Katie, his body language didn't seem all that certain she was guilty of anything, but that could have just been wishful thinking on her part.

When they pulled into the parking lot of the station, he helped her out and escorted her into the same room she had been questioned in earlier, with Officer Fitch following along behind them. She had convinced Officer Beauregard to not officially book her until after he had heard what information she had. Once the three of them were in the room and she had been read her rights — just in case — Katie asked if she could begin.

Officer Beauregard checked his watch. "My shift still has about four hours left, so have at it."

"Envelope, please."

Chapter 10

The Detail

KATIE OPENED THE ENVELOPE AND PULLED OUT THE paperwork with both her handwriting and that of Linda, where she had added information as Katie was getting ready to leave.

"I know it's not much, but I did find two other witnesses that heard an argument between two men in the park. One of them, John, also couldn't make out anything the men said, but the woman on the second floor, Myrtle, she woke to the sounds of the argument as well. The only word she heard clearly was cliff. Now, I've asked around and couldn't find anyone who knew of any cliffs in the area with a reputation for *accidents*." She put air quotes around accidents. "I did ask more questions about Mr. Frazellie and his daughter, Jessie. Seems that her mother disappeared when Jessie was very young and he later ended up with the second marriage to Stephanie, and that's how he had the four young children."

"Katie, the way you spoke earlier, I assumed you had some evidence that I would want."

"I think you will want this, but I need to make sure you have all the information before you arrest the correct person."

"Let me guess, you don't think the correct person is you, do you?"

"I can't think of a single reason why you would suspect me. I have no motive. My visit has been very successful, even with Scoop of the Day open and operational. I've never met Mr. Frazellie before Thursday. I can't say that I had an opportunity. I heard the argument, which two other people also heard, and shortly after, I came out of the truck to the two of you already on the scene of a murder. How did you learn about the murder, anyway?" Katie didn't realize it, but there was no reason for them to happen across a dead body in the middle of the night. Even if they were patrolling in their cars, there's no way they would have seen him in the fountain in the middle of the park.

"Not that I need to answer you, but we had an anonymous tip. Someone called it into the non-emergency number."

"Feel free to check my phone."

"You could have a secondary phone. If you were feeling guilty about what you had done, you still could have made the decision to try not to get caught by avoiding calling your own crime in from your cell phone."

"Noted. Now, means. I'm significantly smaller than Mr. Frazellie. What kind of means would have you believe I killed him? I saw the two marks on his face. I dare say I'd have to stand on a step stool to cause those unless I was swinging a club."

"Officer Fitch found an ice cream scoop not too far from the body."

"With my fingerprints, of course?"

Officer Beauregard toed the floor of the interview room. "We haven't found any prints on it."

"I can't wait to hear what evidence you're planning to use to arrest me then. The murder weapon was an ice cream scoop, so I must have done it? You do know the man who was murdered owned his own ice cream shop, right? Is it just slightly possible, if not probable, that the ice cream scoop was his?"

"It's possible."

"Do you care that I only have plastic scoops in my truck?" Since she hadn't been cuffed, she put her hands on her hips and huffed.

"We have a team searching your truck now?"

"You what? What about Jaspurr? Do they know about Jaspurr? He can't be let out. He's not an outdoor cat." She started to panic and stood, placing her hands flat on the metal table.

"I made sure they knew about Jaspurr. He'll be waiting in an air-conditioned cruiser while they search it."

She sat back down. "So, here is where we talk about what's in the envelope."

Officer Beauregard couldn't contain his impatience. "About time."

"As it turns out, what Myrtle heard had nothing to do with a cliff. When she heard cliff, it was the name Cliff." Katie turned around. "Officer Fitch, would you care to tell me who your mother is?"

Officer Fitch shook his head side to side.

"Cat got your tongue? You know, in all this time, I haven't heard you say a single word. A grunt here or there, but no actual words. After Linda helped me with these names on my list, I started to wonder what your connection to Mr. Frazellie was. Care to tell me about your parents, Cliff Fitch, you know, so Officer Beauregard can arrest the correct person?" She held up a paper with Cliff's name added where Katie had written Officer _____ Fitch.

In the highest pitched male voice Katie could imagine for a man of his size, Officer Cliff Fitch began to answer. "My mother was a woman Walter had an affair with. I was born, and my mom raised me on her own. I didn't find out until recently that Walter was my biological father. Apparently, he didn't know about me either, and when I confronted him, he told me to go jump off a cliff. He thought it was pretty funny that my name was also Cliff. He blamed me for his first wife leaving him. My mom told me recently that she had confronted a woman married to my father, apparently it was Camille, saying she wanted Walter to be in her son's life, and that's why Camille disappeared. We fought about all of it, and I won, the fight, that is."

"Why the ice cream scoop?" asked Katie. Officer

Beauregard was standing, silently, with his mouth hanging open.

"I didn't go there with the intention to kill him. It wasn't premeditated, you've got to believe it. When we got into the physical fight, he took the scoop out of his pocket and tried to hit me with it. I was bigger and stronger and wrestled it from him. I was so angry, I started to hit him with it. After the second blow, he collapsed into the fountain. He must have hit his head because he never got up. I realized how bad it was, wiped down the scoop and chucked it between the fountain and your truck. I wasn't thinking straight."

Officer Beauregard finally moved his feet and approached Cliff. "Cliff Fitch, you're under arrest for the murder of Walter Frazellie." Cliff cooperated as Officer Beauregard manipulated his arms behind his back to put the handcuffs on. They left the room as Officer Beauregard was reading him his rights. The door closed, leaving Katie alone in the interview room. About two minutes later, the front desk clerk came to let her out and tell her she was free to go.

"Can you please tell Officer Beauregard that I'll be at my truck the rest of the day, and he can come get my notes if he wants them?"

"Of course, Ms. Thorne. Did you need a ride back to your ice cream truck?"

"I'd appreciate it."

An officer Katie hadn't met yet drove her back to The Green where her ice cream truck looked just like she left it. "Do you know if they already finished searching my truck?"

"Officer Beauregard hadn't ordered it to be searched yet, so no one touched it."

"Thanks." Katie was released from the back seat of the cruiser and immediately went to check on Jaspurr.

While Jaspurr wasn't in the spot where she left him, he was asleep, only opening one eye when Katie found him on the passenger seat of the truck. She ruffled the fur on top of his head and plopped down in the driver's seat. "It's been a day, Jaspurr. Want a quick walk before I start scooping?" He closed his eye and sighed the way only a spoiled ice-cream-truck cat could. "Suit yourself." She attached his collar to his seatbelt so he couldn't exit the truck while she was working.

Katie stood up and moved to the serving window, opening it in one swift motion. Since the weather had cleared a bit, she spent the next several hours scooping cones and dishes of ice cream for kids in strollers, teens on their bikes and all manner of adults. She ran out of two flavors — Chocolate Mudslide and Mint Chocolate Chip off the Old Block — but had plenty of the rest to finish out the evening.

When the line died down, and she was contemplating closing early, Officer Beauregard pulled up in the cruiser.

"Katie Thorne, what made you think you could solve this murder on your own like that? Were you an investigator or something in a former life?"

"Actually, this is the second murder I have solved,

thank you very much. I don't know what made me think I could do it, but I'm glad that I didn't just leave it up to someone else. Could you imagine being the officer who arrested the ice cream truck lady for murder only to have her sit in jail, go through trial and be found innocent on lack of evidence? That guy would be laughed out of the profession." Her lip quirked up on one side and she stared down at him.

"Message received. Thank you for your help. I still can't believe it was my partner."

"Did he confess to everything after you arrested him?"

"Everything, just the same as the first time, and then some. He was the one who called in the body from a phone he bought from a gas station. We've already recovered it from the rocks along the river where he confessed to tossing it."

Katie held up a pink ice cream scoop made of plastic. "Did you also search Scoop of the Day to see if his ice cream scoops matched the murder weapon?"

"We did, and it did. I already said thank you. You don't need to rub it in."

"Oh, I think I do, just a little bit."

"I can take it."

Katie put the scoop down. "I feel so bad for Jessie. She's lost her father and the brother she never knew she had, all in one weekend."

"She knew Cliff too. They weren't friends or anything, but they were in school together for a year. It's got to be so hard for her to process. Luckily, it seems like

Stephanie is supporting her emotionally, and she's still planning to go to college. They'll close Scoop of the Day early this season and figure out what the family wants to do next summer."

"And what about Walter's other businesses?"

"I've put in some calls to see about his competitors helping take over his clients until Stephanie and Jessie make some decisions. There are a lot of good people who live here and will help out for a bit. If you plan on stopping through next summer, I'm sure it'll be all worked out by then."

"Next summer? Sounds like you just told me this place will need ice cream around Labor Day. I might just be back here sooner than I thought."

Officer Beauregard laughed. "We'll keep in touch about the closing date for Scoop of the Day. How about that?"

"It's a deal. Now, what can I get you?" She pointed to the flavor list. 'I'm out of chocolate and mint chip."

"I'll take a dish of toffee, please."

She scooped and they said goodbye for the night after Katie handed off her envelope of notes. He had her phone number, and she had his, in case they needed anything from each other in the future, though she didn't see herself coming back too soon.

With the truck all locked up and cleaned, she took Jaspurr out for a walk and talk. "Jaspurr, what are your thoughts about visiting Vermont? I hear they've got some great college towns we might want to look into."

Jaspurr rubbed her leg several times with the side of

his face.

"Vermont it is."

Katie and Jaspurr returned to her truck for a final night of sleep in this location. She didn't know what the plan was for tomorrow, but it didn't involve investigating a murder, and that was fine by her.

PLEASE LEAVE A REVIEW!

⭐⭐⭐⭐⭐

Virginia K Bennett

An Appetite for Solving Crime

THANK YOU FOR READING MY BOOK!
I WOULD LOVE TO READ YOUR FEEDBACK ON
FACEBOOK, INSTAGRAM, AMAZON, OR
SIMPLY SEND AN EMAIL TO:
authorvirginiakbennett@gmail.com

Also by Virginia K. Bennett

Ice Cream Truck Mysteries

Chilled to the Bone

* * *

A Newfound Lake Cozy Mystery:

Catch of the Day

A View From The Ledge

Once Inn A Lifetime

Potluck of the Draw

With Sugar on Roundtop

Err on the Side Dish of Caution

Hand Caught in the Christmas Cookie Jar

The Toast of New Year's Eve

Now You Sesame, Now You Don't

Disturbing the Pizza

Maple Fools' Day

Ride Off Into the Cotton Candy Sky

Kiss Your Apps Goodbye

Red, White & Final BBQ

Killer, Killer, Lobster & Chicken Dinner

* * *

The Mysteries of Cozy Cove:

Much Ado About Muffin

It's All or Muffin

Muffin to Lose

Nothing Ventured, Muffin Gained

You Ain't Seen Muffin Yet

Here Goes Muffin

About the Author

When she's not writing on her couch with her two cats, Twyla and Geo, Virginia is busy teaching middle school math, grocery shopping, cooking or spending time with her husband and son. Together, her small family loves to go geocaching and visit theme parks.

Mysteries have always been an interesting challenge for Virginia, much like watching a magician perform. Unless you want to hear the entire thought process behind who she thinks is the killer and why, you might want to avoid watching any movies together.

The path to publishing a book is different for everyone and her path is full of twists and turns. Thank you to those who support the journey.

facebook.com/VirginiaKBennett

instagram.com/authorvkbennett

Made in United States
Cleveland, OH
05 January 2025